P9-DGW-776

Troll
SWAP

FOR eve, tess, Aurora & eLSA...

the goodest good little girls I know.

Copyright © 2013 by Leigh Hodgkinson

Nosy Crow and its logos are trademarks of
Nosy Crow, Ltd. Used under license.

First U.S. edition 2014

Library of Congress Catalog Card Number pending

ISBN 978-0-7636-7101-3

13 14 15 16 17 18 FgF 10 9 8 7 6 5 4 3 2 1

Printed in Shenzhen, guangdong, China

This book was typeset in Public.
The illustrations were done in mixed media.

Nosy Crow
An imprint of
Candlewick Press
99 Dover Street
Somerville, Massachusetts 02144

www.nosycrow.com
www.candlewick.com

Troll
SWAP

nosy crow

An imprint of Candlewick Press

Leigh
HODGKINSON

Say hello to

Timothy Limpet.

Timothy Limpet is a hairy troll
who lives somewhere far away.

Trolls are messy, mucky creatures. Trolls live in damp, dark, squelchy caves. Trolls love scaring the heebie-jeebies out of anyone they can.

Timothy Limpet is **not** like other trolls. Timothy Limpet is **nice** and **polite** and **tidy**. Timothy Limpet's **cave** is not at all damp, dark, or squelchy, thank you very much.

The other trolls
think that Timothy Limpet
is a particularly terrible troll and
not at all like them.

Meanwhile . . . somewhere else . . .

Say hello to

Tabitha Lumpit.

Tabitha Lumpit is a little girl who lives in a house with her mommy and daddy.

Most little boys and girls are nice.

Most little boys and girls are polite.

Most little boys and girls are tidy.

Tabitha Lumpit is **not** like
other little boys and girls.

Tabitha Lumpit is loud and loopy and messy. Tabitha Lumpit has a laugh like a giant foghorn. Tabitha Lumpit would rather pick her nose than a flower any day of the week.

When Tabitha Lumpit sees a muddy puddle . . .

she cannot stop herself from jumping in it and making a super-splashy muddy mess.

All Tabitha Lumpit's mommy and daddy want is for her to be nice and polite and tidy, just like them.

Being like most other little boys and girls is almost **impossible**, thinks Tabitha Lumpit.

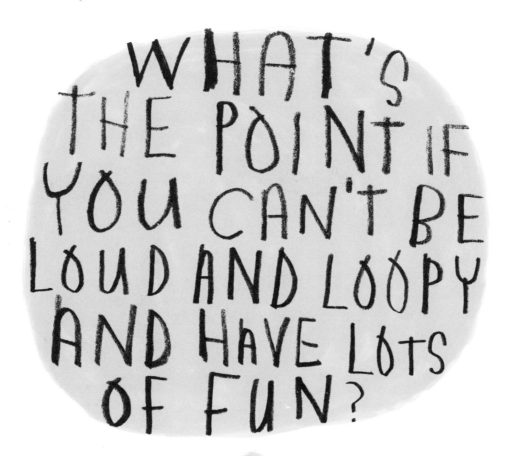

WHAT'S THE POINT IF YOU CAN'T BE LOUD AND LOOPY AND HAVE LOTS OF FUN?

And being a disgusting troll just isn't as easy as it looks, thinks Timothy Limpet.

But then something happened that changed **everything.** Tabitha and Timothy were not looking where they were going when . . .

CLONK!

Tabitha Lumpit said hello to Timothy Limpet.
And Timothy Limpet said hello to Tabitha Lumpit.

HELLO! I AM A GOOD LITTLE GIRL NAMED TABITHA LUMPIT—AND WHO ARE YOU?

Hello! I am a big, scary troll named Timothy Limpet.

YOU DON'T SEEM VERY TROLLISH. YOU SEEM NICE AND POLITE AND TIDY – A BIT LIKE I AM SUPPOSED TO BE.

said Tabitha.

And you don't seem very good-little-girlish. You seem loud and loopy and messy — why, a bit like I am supposed to be,

said Timothy.

This gave them both a SWAPPINGLY good idea . . . .

so they swapped places! The other trolls were amazed by what a first-class troll Timothy had become.

And Tabitha's mommy and daddy couldn't believe what a nice and polite and tidy little girl Tabitha was.

But after a while, the other trolls began to miss the **old** Timothy Limpet.

SPLOSH

YUCK!

CRACK

CRUNCH

WHIFF

THUNK

Somehow, things just **weren't** the same.

And Tabitha Lumpit's mommy and daddy
soon started to miss the OLD Tabitha.

Now life seemed just a tiny bit DULL.

Timothy found that once everything was squeaky-clean, he soon got a bit thumb-twiddly.

B<u>o</u>r<u>i</u><u>n</u>g<u>!</u>

Here, everyone was nice and polite and tidy, just like him. Here, he simply wasn't special at all.

And Tabitha found that picking her nose, being loud and messy, and jumping in squelchy mud didn't surprise anybody. Here, that was just ordinary.

BORING!

They both **knew** that there was only one thing to do.

It was time to swap back
and for both of them to
go home, where they

belonged.

And they all lived **happily** . . .

and **LOOPiLY** ever after.